Boots
for Beth

Boots
for Beth

Alex Moran

**Illustrated by
Lisa Campbell Ernst**

Green Light Readers
Harcourt, Inc.

Orlando Austin New York San Diego Toronto London

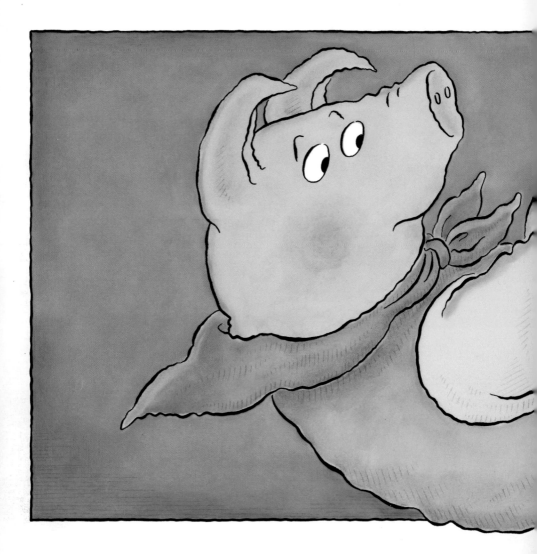

Beth was sad.

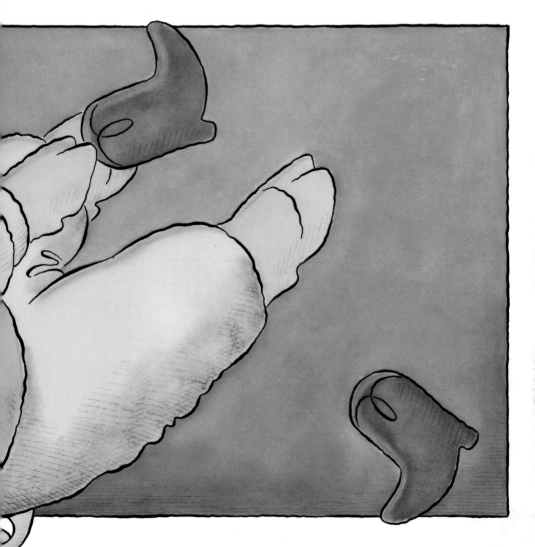

"My red boots don't fit," she cried.
"I cannot get them on."

"Could you use my boots?" asked Meg.

"Too big," said Beth.

"Will my boots fit?" asked Ned.

"Too small," said Beth.

"Could you use my boots?" asked Liz.

"Too soft," said Beth.

"Will my boots help?" asked Ted.

"Too wet," said Beth.

"Can you put on my boot?" asked Jeff.

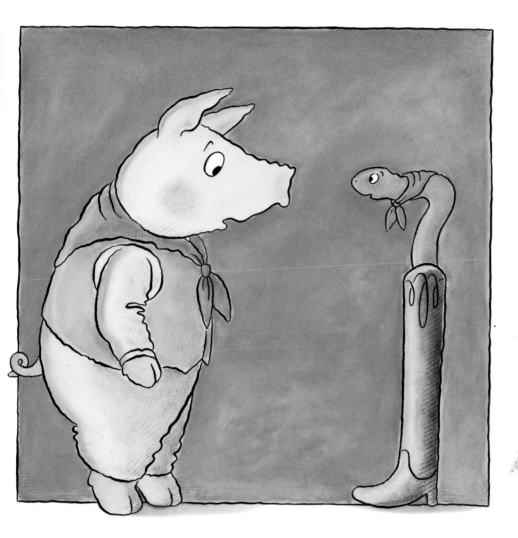

"Too thin," said Beth.

Beth still felt sad.
Her friends all felt bad.

Then they found a
big surprise for Beth.

"New red boots," said Beth.
"Thanks!"

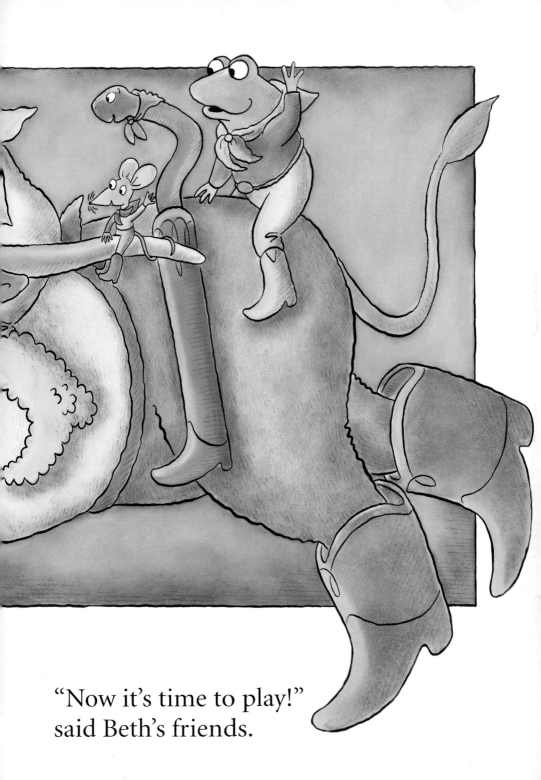

"Now it's time to play!"
said Beth's friends.

Think About It

1. What problem does Beth have?

2. How is Beth's problem solved?

3. What happens first in the story? What happens last?

4. How can you tell that Beth's friends are nice?

5. Have you ever had a problem like Beth's? What did you do?

Shoes Around the World

paper

crayons or markers

1. Draw a picture of your favorite shoes.

2. Look at pictures of people who live around the world. Draw pictures of what they wear on their feet.

Who wears shoes that look like yours?

Meet the Illustrator

Lisa Campbell Ernst got the idea for *Boots for Beth* while shopping for shoes with her two children. "How sad we feel when a favorite pair of shoes no longer fits," she says. "Then the search for just the right new pair begins. Some shoes are too big, too small, too stiff. At last you find just the right ones!"

Lisa Campbell Ernst

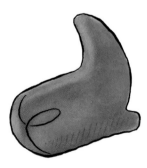

www.HarcourtBooks.com

First Green Light Readers edition 2002
Green Light Readers is a trademark of Harcourt, Inc., registered in the
United States of America and/or other jurisdictions.

The Library of Congress has cataloged an earlier edition as follows:
Moran, Alex.
Boots for Beth/written by Alex Moran; illustrated by Lisa Campbell Ernst.
p. cm.
"Green Light Readers."
Summary: When Beth the pig's favorite boots become too small, her friends help
her find the perfect new pair.
[1. Boots—Fiction. 2. Pigs—Fiction. 3. Animals—Fiction.] I. Title. II. Series.
PZ7.M788193Bo 2002
[E]—dc21 2001002417
ISBN 0-15-204878-2
ISBN 0-15-204838-3 (pb)

A C E G H F D B
A C E G H F D B (pb)

Ages 5–7
Grades: 1–2
Guided Reading Level: G–H
Reading Recovery Level: 12

Green Light Readers
For the reader who's ready to GO!

Five Tips to Help Your Child Become a Great Reader

1. Get involved. Reading aloud to and with your child is just as important as encouraging your child to read independently.

2. Be curious. Ask questions about what your child is reading.

3. Make reading fun. Allow your child to pick books on subjects that interest her or him.

4. Words are everywhere—not just in books. Practice reading signs, packages, and cereal boxes with your child.

5. Set a good example. Make sure your child sees YOU reading.

Why Green Light Readers Is the Best Series for Your New Reader

• Created exclusively for beginning readers by some of the biggest and brightest names in children's books

• Reinforces the reading skills your child is learning in school

• Encourages children to read—and finish—books by themselves

• Offers extra enrichment through fun, age-appropriate activities unique to each story

• Incorporates characteristics of the Reading Recovery program used by educators

• Developed with Harcourt School Publishers and credentialed educational consultants

Daniel's Mystery Egg
Alma Flor Ada/G. Brian Karas

Animals on the Go
Jessica Brett/Richard Cowdrey

Marco's Run
Wesley Cartier/Reynold Ruffins

Digger Pig and the Turnip
Caron Lee Cohen/Christopher Denise

Tumbleweed Stew
Susan Stevens Crummel/Janet Stevens

The Chick That Wouldn't Hatch
Claire Daniel/Lisa Campbell Ernst

Splash!
Ariane Dewey/Jose Aruego

Get That Pest!
Erin Douglas/Wong Herbert Yee

Why the Frog Has Big Eyes
Betsy Franco/Joung Un Kim

I Wonder
Tana Hoban

A Bed Full of Cats
Holly Keller

The Fox and the Stork
Gerald McDermott

Boots for Beth
Alex Moran/Lisa Campbell Ernst

Catch Me If You Can!
Bernard Most

The Very Boastful Kangaroo
Bernard Most

Farmers Market
Carmen Parks/Edward Martinez

Shoe Town
Janet Stevens/Susan Stevens Crummel

The Enormous Turnip
Alexei Tolstoy/Scott Goto

Where Do Frogs Come From?
Alex Vern

The Purple Snerd
Rozanne Lanczak Williams/
Mary GrandPré

Look for more Green Light Readers wherever books are sold!